Going for a SEA BATH

Written by **Andrée Poulin**
Illustrated by **Anne-Claire Delisle**
Translated by Erin Woods

pajamapress

First published in Canada and the United States in 2016
Text copyright © 2016 Andrée Poulin
Illustration copyright © 2016 Anne-Claire Delisle
This edition copyright © 2016 Pajama Press Inc.
Translated from the French by Erin Woods
First published in French by Dominique et compagnie

10 9 8 7 6 5 4 3 2 1

www.pajamapress.ca   info@pajamapress.ca

 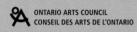
Canada Council   Conseil des arts
for the Arts   du Canada

ONTARIO ARTS COUNCIL
CONSEIL DES ARTS DE L'ONTARIO   Canadä
an Ontario government agency
un organisme du gouvernement de l'Ontario

The publisher gratefully acknowledges the support of the Canada Council
for the Arts and the Ontario Arts Council for its publishing program. We
acknowledge the financial support of the Government of Canada through
the Canada Book Fund (CBF) for our publishing activities.

Library and Archives Canada Cataloguing in Publication
Poulin, Andrée [Bain trop plein! English]
     Going for a sea bath / written by Andrée Poulin ; illustrated by
Anne-Claire Delisle ; translated by Erin Woods.
Translation of: Un bain trop plein! ISBN 978-1-927485-92-7 (bound)
     I. Delisle, Anne-Claire, illustrator II. Woods, Erin V., translator
III. Title. IV. Title: Bain trop plein! English.
PS8581.O837B3413 2016   jC843'.54   C2015-905271-8

Publisher Cataloging-in-Publication Data (U.S.)
Poulin, Andrée.
  Going for a sea bath / written by Andrée Poulin ; illustrated by Anne-
Claire Delisle ; translated by Erin Woods.
Originally published in Saint-Lamberg, Québec: Dominique et compagnie,
as Un bain trop plein.
[32] pages : color illustrations ; cm.
Summary: "When Leanne complains that bath time is boring, her father
has the great idea to bring her a sea turtle as a companion. As her father
has more excellent, fabulous, and spectacular ideas, the bathtub soon
overflows with sea creatures. Leanne resolves the problem with an idea of
her own: she will have her bath in the sea, which is never boring at all" –
Provided by publisher.
ISBN-13: 978-1-927485-92-7
1. Baths -- Juvenile fiction. 2. Baths, Sea – Juvenile fiction. 3. Seashore
animals -- Juvenile fiction. 4. Fathers and daughters – Juvenile fiction. I.
Title. II. Delisle, Anne-Claire. III. Woods, Erin.
[E] dc23   PZ7.P685Go 2016

Manufactured by Sheck Wah Tong Printing Ltd.
Printed in Hong Kong, China

Pajama Press Inc.
181 Carlaw Ave. Suite 207 Toronto, Ontario Canada, M4M 2S1

Distributed in Canada by UTP Distribution
5201 Dufferin Street Toronto, Ontario Canada, M3H 5T8

Distributed in the U.S. by Ingram Publisher Services
1 Ingram Blvd. La Vergne, TN 37086, USA

To the real Léanne
—Andrée

To Gaspar, who loves
to splash in his bath
—Anne-Claire

"Leanne, come take your bath!"
"I don't want a bath!" grumbled Leanne.
"It's so boring! It's annoying! It's a pain!"
"If you never take a bath, you will smell like a skunk," said her father.
"But there's nothing to play with in the bath," said Leanne.

Her father cried, "**I have a good idea!**"

Leanne's father ran all the way to the sea.
He brought back **one turtle**.
Leanne tickled the turtle under his shell.
Then she said, "He doesn't do much."

Her father cried, "**I have a great idea!**"

Leanne's father ran all the way to the sea. He brought back **two eels**. Leanne watched the eels zigzag through the water. Then she said, "These eels are too dark."

Her father cried, "**I have an excellent idea!**"

Leanne's father ran all the way to the sea.
He brought back **three clown fish**.
The fish swam between Leanne's toes.
She burst out laughing. "That tickles!"
Then she said, "It would be even better if
there were more of them."

Her father cried, "**Terrific idea!**"

Leanne's father ran all the way to the sea.
He brought back **four seahorses**.
When Leanne sang to them, the seahorses
started dancing. She exclaimed, "Taking a
bath is exciting! It's the best!"
Leanne's father smiled. When his daughter
was happy, it made him feel like dancing.

Then Leanne said, "It would be even more fun
if there were more animals."

Her father cried, "**Brilliant idea!**"

Leanne's father ran all the way to the sea.
He brought back **five shrimps**.
Leanne looked closely at one shrimp's head.
"Their eyes are as round as candies!" Then she
said, "What if we invite the shrimps' cousins?"

Her father cried, **"Marvelous idea!"**

Leanne's father ran all the way to the sea.
He brought back **six hermit crabs**.

The crustaceans walked backwards through the bathtub.
Leanne laughed. "They are crashing into everything."

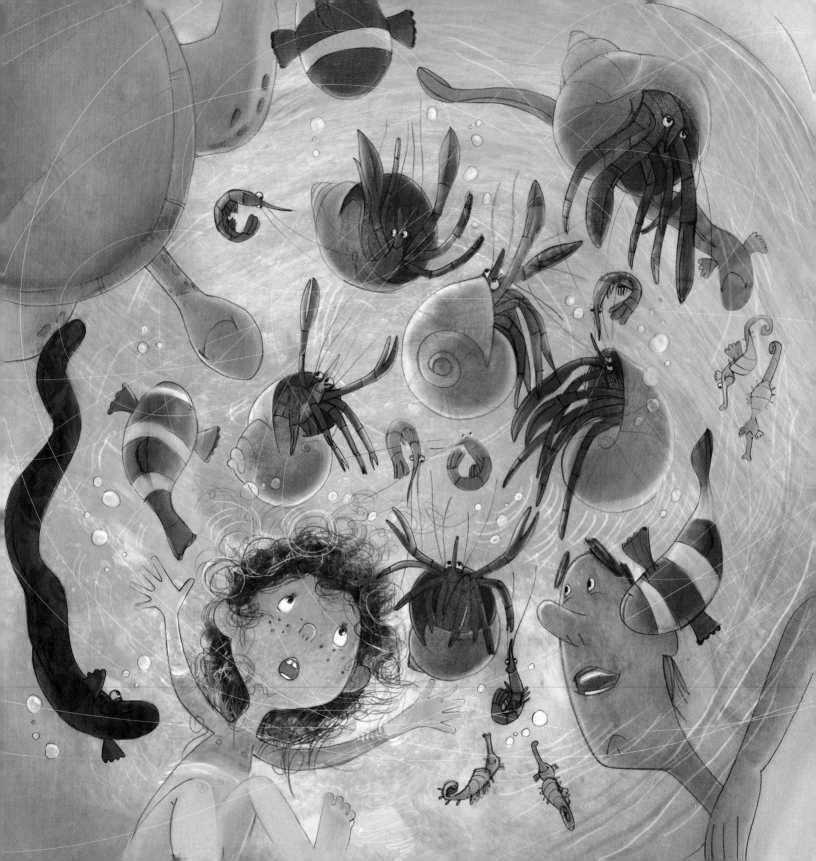

Leanne's father asked, "If you have five shrimps and six hermit crabs, how many legs is that?"

"Too many legs!" his daughter said. Then she suggested, "What if we add some animals with **no** legs?"

Her father cried, "**Magnificent idea!**"

Leanne's father ran all the way to the sea.
He brought back **seven sea urchins**.

Leanne lined the edge of the bathtub with a
sea-urchin garland. Then she said, "It would be
even more lovely with more decorations."

Her father cried, "**Phenomenal idea!**"

Leanne's father ran all the way to the sea.
He brought back **eight anemones**.
Leanne placed one anemone between
each sea urchin. Then she said, "I think
we are still missing something."

Her father cried, "**I have a spectacular idea!**"

Leanne's father ran all the way to the sea.
He brought back **nine starfish.**
Leanne tried to place the starfish between
the sea urchins and the anemones.
Impossible!

The eels, clown fish, sea horses, shrimps, and
hermit crabs started wriggling and writhing.
Even the big turtle was on the move.
"I don't have enough arms to organize
all this!" said Leanne.

Her father cried,
"I have a super-stupendous idea!"

Leanne's father ran all the way to the sea.
He brought back **ten octopi**.
Leanne tried to count their arms. She could
not do it. There were too, too many arms.

In the bathtub, creatures were jiggling and jostling. What a mess!
Leanne shook her head.
"My bath is overflowing," she said.
"What should we do?" asked her father.

Then Leanne cried, **"I have an absolutely extraordinary idea!"**

Leanne and her father ran all
the way to the sea.
The waves were **wonderful**.
The sun was **superb**.
The sand was **sublime**.
Leanne said, "A sea bath is
the most fun of all!"